THE SORCERER'S MAZE
TIME MACHINE

by

Blair Polly & DM Potter

YouSayWhichWay.com

ISBN-13: 978-1546362173

ISBN-10: 1546362177

THE SORCERER'S MAZE
TIME MACHINE

How This Book Works

This is an interactive book with YOU as the main character. You have entered the sorcerer's maze and have to find your way out again by answering questions and solving riddles.

You say which way the story goes. Some paths will lead you into trouble, but they all lead to discovery and adventure.

Have fun and follow the links of your choice. For example, **P34** means to turn to page 34. Or at any time, you can go to the List of Choices on **P104** and choose a section from there.

Can you find your way through the maze? The only way to find out is to get reading!

Oh … and watch out for avalanches!

In the laboratory

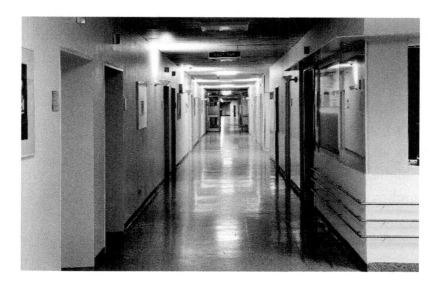

The door is ajar so Matilda gives it a shove and walks into the laboratory. "Hey," she says over her shoulder, "come and look at this."

"Are we allowed?" you ask, stepping cautiously through the doorway. "This area's probably off limits."

"I didn't see a sign," Matilda says, rubbing a finger along the edge of a stainless steel bench as she proceeds further into the brightly lit room. "And if they're going to leave the door open…"

Matilda is an Australian foreign exchange student at your school. She's adventurous and sometimes a little crazy, but she's interesting and the two of you have become good friends.

The rest of your classmates are back in the cafeteria questioning the tour guide about the research facility while they wait for lunch to be served. When Matilda suggested a quick walk, you never guessed she planned to snoop around.

The lab's benches are crammed with electrical equipment. Wires and cables run like spaghetti between servers and fancy hardware. Lights and gauges flicker and glow.

You move a little further into the room. "What do you think all this stuff does?"

Matilda wanders down the narrow space between two benches, looking intently at the equipment as she goes. "I dunno. But they don't skimp on gear, do they?"

A low hum buzzes throughout the room. Most of the components are large and expensive looking. But near the end of one bench, Matilda spots a few smaller pieces of tech.

She prods a brick-sized black box with a row of green numbers glowing across it. "I wonder what this does." She picks it up.

Tiny lights glow above a circular dial. On the top of the box is an exposed circuit board made of copper and green plastic.

"Looks like an old digital clock," you say pointing at the first number in the row. "See here's the hours and minutes, then the day, the month and the year." You pull out your cell phone and check the time. "Yep. It's spot on."

"That makes sense," Matilda says. "But what's the dial for?"

"Beats me. To set an alarm, maybe?

Matilda rubs her finger along a curved piece of copper tubing fitted neatly into one end of the box. "So what's this coil for? Doesn't look like any timer I've ever seen."

When she turns the box over, there is a sticky label on its bottom. It reads:

Hands Off - Property of the Sorcerer

"Who's the sorcerer?" Matilda asks.

You shrug. "A scientist maybe?"

"A sorcerer's a magician, not a scientist." She turns the box back over and starts fiddling with the dial.

You take a step back. "I don't think that's a good—"

A sudden burst of static crackles through the air. The copper coil glows bright red and there's a high-pitched squeal.

FLASH—BANG!

Pink mist fills the air.

"Crikey!" Matilda says. "What the heck caused that?"

Matilda looms ghostlike through the haze.

"We're in for it now," you say, hoping the smoke alarm doesn't go off. "Someone must have heard that."

But as the mist clears, someone hearing you is the last of your worries. "Where—where's the lab gone?"

You're standing on an open plain, brown and burnt by the blistering sun.

In the distance three huge stone structures rise above the shimmering heat haze. Workers swarm over the site like ants on piles of sugar.

Matilda stares, her mouth open, trying to make sense of it all. The black box dangles from her hand. She turns to face you. "Streuth mate! The lab. She—she's completely disappeared!"

"But how? Unless…" You reach down and lift the box so you can check the numbers flashing on its side. "This says it's 11:45."

Matilda nods. "Yeah, that's about right. Just before lunch."

"In the year 2560!"

Matilda's eyes widen. "2560? How can that be?"

"That's 2560 BC," a voice behind you says. "See the little minus sign in front of the numbers?"

The two of you spin around.

"Jeez, mate," Matilda says, glaring at the newcomer. "Where the blazes did you spring from? You nearly scared last night's dinner outta me."

The owner of the voice is a boy about your age, dressed in white cotton.

Bands of gold encircle his wrists. His hair is jet black and cut straight across in the front, like his barber put a bowl on his head and used it as a guide.

"I'm the sorcerer's apprentice," he says with a smile. "You've been playing with the sorcerer's time machine haven't you?"

"Time machine?" you and Matilda say in unison.

The apprentice nods. "Welcome to ancient Egypt. The pyramids are coming along nicely don't you think?"

You glance over towards the structures in the distance then back to the boy. "But how did we—"

"— end up here?" the apprentice says. "When you fiddled with the sorcerer's machine, you bent space-time. In fact you bent it so much, you've ended up in the sorcerer's maze. Now you've got to answer questions and riddles to get out."

Matilda's upper lip curls and her eyes squint, contorting her face into a look of total confusion. "What sorta questions?"

The apprentice reaches out his hand. "Don't worry. The questions aren't difficult. But first you'd better give me that box, before you get yourself in trouble."

"Is answering questions the only way to get back?" you ask.

The boy in white nods then gives you a smile. "Here's how the time maze works. If you answer a question correctly, you get to move closer to your own time. But if you get it wrong. I spin the dial and we take our chances."

You gulp. "You mean we could end up anywhere?"

"You mean any-when, don't ya?" Matilda says.

The sorcerer's apprentice chuckles. "I suppose you're right. Anywhere, anytime. It's all the same in the sorcerer's maze."

"But we've got to answer questions to get home?" you repeat. "There's no other way?"

"Sorry, I don't make the rules. I just do what the sorcerer says. At least he's sent me along to help out. That's some consolation, eh?"

"Well… I suppose…"

"Get on with it then," Matilda says in her typical no-nonsense way. "I'm hungry and it's nearly lunchtime."

The boy tucks the black box under his arm, then reaches into a fold of his robe and pulls out a scroll of papyrus. He straightens the scroll and reads. "Okay here goes. The pyramids are about 481 feet high but they weren't used as look out posts or land marks. What was their purpose?" The apprentice looks at you expectantly.

It's time for your first decision.

6

Which do you choose?
The pyramids were used as accommodation for slaves?
P8
Or
The pyramids were used as tombs? **P11**

Stop. You need to go back and make a choice. That is how you'll work your way through the sorcerer's maze.

The pyramids were used as accommodation for slaves

"Oops," the sorcerer's apprentice says. "I'm afraid to say that isn't the right answer. But don't worry, we'll spin the dial and see where we end up eh? Pity I was hoping to have a little look at how the Egyptians lifted up those big blocks of stone.

The boy reaches for the dial on the front of the box.

"Hey wait!" you shout. "You sure you couldn't give me another chance?"

The boy shakes his head. "If it were up to me, I wouldn't have a problem. But I don't make the rules."

He spins the dial. The air crackles.

FLASH—BANG!

That pink mist is back. You wave you hand in front of your face to fan it away.

"Crikey!" Matilda says, fanning like crazy. "Look over there! It's the Eiffel Tower!"

She's right. You'd know that shape anywhere.

You turn to the sorcerer's apprentice. "But—but where's the top of it?

"The French haven't finished it yet," the sorcerer's apprentice says.

He's now dressed in a black frock coat that hangs nearly to his knees. Under the coat charcoal-colored pin-striped pants meet shiny black shoes with silver buckles. On top of his head is a top hat, and he carries a cane. He studies the front of the box and points at the last four numbers. "See, it's only 1888."

"1888?" you say. "At least we're closer to home. That's good."

The boy smiles, "Did you know that the four legs of the tower point north, south, east and west?"

"Like a compass?" Matilda asks.

The apprentice nods "It's being built for the Exposition Universelle of 1889. It won't be finished until March next year."

"Exposition Univer—"

"—it's like a World Fair," the boys says. "Did you know the Eiffel Tower has over two and half million rivets?"

You remember reading something about that. "Didn't the French build the Statue of Liberty too?"

"That's right," the apprentice says. "So, are you ready for another question?"

"Heck yeah," Matilda says. "My stomach's rumbling. We haven't had lunch yet."

"Okay, here we go," the boy says, pulling a piece of paper from his coat pocket. "In what year was George Washington, the first president of the United States, elected?"

"Jeez mate. How am I supposed to know that?" Matilda moans. "Why don't ya ask us something 'bout Australia? Then I might be able to help."

The boy smiles. "Maybe. But hey, even a guess has a 50/50 chance."

Then he turns to you. "Which do you choose?"

Washington was elected in 1689? **P14**

Or

Washington was elected in 1789? **P16**

The pyramids were used as tombs

"Well done," the sorcerer's apprentice says. "That's correct. The pyramids were used as burial chambers for Egyptian kings and queens. They were filled with all the things the Egyptians believed people would need in the afterlife."

Matilda gives you a smile. "I knew that."

"So what now?" you ask the boy. "We get to head towards home, right?"

"Don't you want to look around?" the boy asks.

"Can we get some food?" Matilda says. "My stomach is rumbling."

"I'm pretty sure we can find something," the boy says.

But then, out of the haze, a group of Egyptian men armed with spears, come running towards you.

They are shouting words you can't understand and they

don't look friendly.

The boy nods and reaches towards the dial on the black box. "I think we'd better get going. How about 1863?"

"Is that an important date?" Matilda asks, casting a glance at the approaching men. "It sounds familiar."

"You'll see," the apprentice says. "You might want to put your hands over your ears," the boy says. "These bangs can damage your hearing after a while."

FLASH—BANG!

Egypt is gone. As the pink cloud thins, you see a big white house across a large expanse of lawn. Two white pillars sit either side of the entrance.

"This mist tastes like cherry," Matilda says, licking her lips. "Yummo!"

You ignore Matilda as she slurps at the air. "So is this 1863?" you ask.

"That's right," the apprentice says. "We're in Washington D.C."

"So that's the White House?" Matilda asks.

"Very good," the apprentice says. "Guess who's president?"

You shrug. "How should I know? That was a long time ago."

"It was Lincoln," the apprentice says, "And what did Abraham Lincoln do that people remember him for?"

"Hang on mate!" Matilda says. "If we're going to answer your questions, we should get to move closer to home. Otherwise we're working for nothing."

"Okay," the apprentice says. "Tell me what Lincoln was famous for and we'll turn the dial nearer your own time. Was it:"

Being the first president to send a man into space? **P18**

Or

Being the president that ended slavery in the United States? **P20**

Washington was elected in 1689

The sorcerer's apprentice frowns. "How could George Washington have been elected in 1689 when the *Declaration of Independence* wasn't signed until 1776? You didn't think that one through did you?"

Matilda frowns. "Hey mate! How were we supposed to know that? It's ancient history. Give us something a bit more recent why don't ya?"

"Yeah," you agree. "Give us a chance or we'll never get home."

The sorcerer's apprentice scratches his head. "Okay, I suppose questions from that long ago are a bit unfair. I'll tell you what. If you promise not to tell the sorcerer. I'll let you have that one over again."

Matilda smiles and gives the apprentice a thumbs up

signal. "Cheers, mate. You're a good sort."

The apprentice reads the last question over. "So which do you choose this time?"

Washington was elected in 1689 **P14**

Or

Washington was elected in 1789? **P16**

Washington was elected in 1789

"Correct," the apprentice says. "How could Washington have been elected in 1689? That's before the United States was even a country."

Matilda gives you a toothy grin. "Good picking, cobber!"

The apprentice turns to you for a translation.

"Cobber means friend," you say.

The sorcerer's apprentice files the information away for future use and then continues his history lesson. "Did you know that Washington served as general and commander-in-chief in the War of Independence against the British, and that he was a slave owner?"

"Really?" you ask. "A slave owner while he was president?"

"Of course we know better now," the apprentice says.

Matilda kicks the ground. "So where are we off to now? I don't suppose they've invented hamburgers yet?"

The sorcerer's apprentice smiles. "No. That wasn't until the 1880s in Texas."

"Well that's closer to our time," Matilda says, turning to you. "What do you reckon?"

You must admit, a burger and fries sounds pretty good right now. "Can we?" you ask the apprentice.

"Sure we can," he says. "Or we can go to 2040. That's a little bit past your time, but it's closer."

"Bleeding heck!" Matilda says. "You mean we can go into the future too?"

The sorcerer's apprentice nods. "But do you want to risk it?" he says with a big grin.

Matilda gives the apprentice a serious look. "Will they have hamburgers in the future too?"

The apprentice grins. "They might."

It is time to make a decision. Which do you choose?

Go to Texas 1880 for burgers? **P23**

Or

Go check out the future? **P31**

Lincoln sent the first man into space

Everything is dark, and the air is thick with the smell of unwashed bodies. Where are Matilda and the boy? "Hello? Anyone there?"

You hear the hollow slap of water against wood.

As your eyes adjust to the dim light, you see vague shapes lying around the floor. You feel yourself rocking to and fro. The stench is horrible. People moan and groan all around you.

"Hello?" you say again. "Matilda? Apprentice? Are you here?"

"Crikey, it stinks worse that the south end of a north-bound dingo," Matilda says. "Get us out of here!"

People mumble in a language you can't understand and water drips on you from above.

"Well that was clever," the boy says from the gloom. "We've ended up in the hold of a slave ship."

"Why?" you ask.

"Because you got that last question wrong! Lincoln abolished slavery in 1862. Man didn't go into space until 1961. What were you thinking?"

You're quite pleased you haven't have lunch. The smell is so bad you'd only throw it up anyway. It's no wonder so many slaves died on the voyage across the Atlantic Ocean, this place is disgusting, and heart breaking.

"Can you ask another question so we can get everyone out of here?" you ask the apprentice.

The boy shakes his head. "Unfortunately no. I'm going to leave, but you have to stay here. Slaves can't just run away. They are trapped for life, and so are you.

"What do you mean? We have to stay here?" you ask in a panic. "Can't you take us with you?"

"Bleedin' heck! You must be joking!" Matilda yells.

"I'm sorry. You've made a bad decision. There's nothing I can do.

The air crackles with electricity. Then there's a FLASH—BANG and the apprentice is gone.

"So what do we do now?" Matilda says.

"I don't—" You see a familiar shape on the floor and reach for it. "Look Matilda, the time machine. He must have dropped it." You lift it to your face and peer at the numbers on its front. You fiddle with the dial. "It's jammed! I can only get two dates."

"Just pick one! Anywhere's got to be better than here," she says.

So which date do you choose?

Do you pick the year 1980? **P26**

Or

Do you pick the year 2040? **P31**

Lincoln ended slavery in the U.S.

The sorcerer's apprentice gives you a smile. "That's right. Slavery officially ended in the United States when the 13th amendment to the constitution was passed in 1865. Now we get to move closer to your time."

"Hey, mate," Matilda says to the apprentice. "How about sending us somewhere interesting for a change? All this history is boring me rigid."

The apprentice shoots Matilda a look, and then turns towards you. "Is that how you feel too?"

You're not sure how to react. Is this a trick? Will the apprentice send you off somewhere dangerous if you say something wrong? "Well I'm not sure…"

The apprentice tucks the black box under his arm and reaches for his pocket. "I'll tell you what, get this next question right and we'll go somewhere you're both sure to like. Sound fair?"

You nod. "Sounds fair."

The apprentice holds up the questions and starts to read. "Wow, this one's a bit tricky."

"Really? Can't you give us an easy one?" you ask.

The apprentice shakes his head. "Sorry, I've got to read them as they come out."

"Well get it over with then, mate." Matilda growls. "No point hanging around like a bad smell."

"Yeah, at least we have a 50/50 chance of getting it right," you say.

"Not this time," the apprentice says, shaking his head slightly. "More like a 25 percent chance. There are four possible answers."

Matilda frowns. "Jeez, mate. That's lower than a snake's armpit."

The apprentice looks at Matilda, then to you. "Translation?"

"Mean trick. She's not happy."

"Well I can't help what comes out of my pocket. Still, if you get this one right, you can go have ice cream. That should cheer you both up.

"And if we get it wrong?" you ask

"You're in for a surprise. Now think carefully and tell me what a 'spiny lumpsucker' is?"

"A spiny lumpsucker?" you say. "Is that really a thing?"

"Sure is," the apprentice says.

You can almost see the steam coming out of Matilda's ears. "What the heck's a spiny lumpsucker?"

"Exactly my question," the apprentice says, turning to you. "So, what do you say? Oh but be careful. If you answer wrong, I'll have to send you back to the start or way off into the future. But, if you get it right, you'll get ice cream!"

Your stomach rumbles at the thought of ice cream.

It is time to make a decision. Is a spiny lumpsucker:

A type of frog? **P1**

A piece of medical equipment? **P31**

A type of fish? **P49**

Or

A slave owner? **P62**

Have a Texan hamburger

When the pink mist clears you feel the sun beating down. The day is hot and dry. You are standing outside a lunch bar in Athens, Texas. The wind whistles down a near empty street.

"Welcome to 1860," the sorcerer's apprentice says, tipping his cowboy hat. "Ya'll come on in and grab some food." He points to a set of swinging doors that lead into a modest restaurant. Inside, wooden stools line a long counter, and sawdust covers the floor.

As you enter, a dark-haired man with a large moustache stands behind the counter. "Howdy folks," he says.

"We'd like to order some lunch," the apprentice says.

"Sure, no problem. Would you like to try my newest invention?" the man says. "I call it the hamburger."

"I'm in," you say.

The three of you sit along the counter. The smell of food cooking makes your mouth water.

"I'm so hungry I could eat road kill," Matilda says, licking her lips.

The man behind the counter looks confused. "Road kill?"

"Thank you, mister," the sorcerer's apprentice says, distracting the man. "We'll have three of your hamburgers please. And some water if we may."

"All righty then. Three hamburgers a comin' up."

After the man goes out back, the apprentice turns to Matilda. "Road kill in 1860? Do you think they run over rabbits with their horses?"

Matilda's face reddens. "Yeah, well…"

The man is back with three glasses of water. "Here you go," the man says, inspecting your clothes. "You kids aren't from around these parts, are you?"

"I'm from Australia," Matilda says. "I'm going to school—"

"—her parents are teachers over in Austin," the apprentice says, butting in.

The man twiddles his moustache. "Australia. Yeah I heard of that. Knew a man headed there to search for gold."

The man goes to the grill and gets busy frying up three juicy patties. Once they've had time to cook, he puts each patty between two thick slabs of bread with fried onion and adds slices of pickle to decorate the side of the plate.

Matilda's eyes widen.

The burgers are so big, and the bread so thick, you wonder if you'll even be able to finish yours.

Matilda has no such doubt and digs right in.

A while later, the three of you are licking your fingers and wiping your hands on cloth napkins. The sorcerer's apprentice pulls a question out of his pocket. "I suppose we'd better get going before someone else gets nosey. You ready for your next question?"

You burp loudly then nod. "Sure. Go for it."

The apprentice reaches for a question. "Ahem…" he says clearing his throat. "Right, here we go. Which of the following is the correct spelling for Matilda's homeland? Be careful with this one, because you might have to go back to the very beginning of the maze if you get it wrong."

Is it:

Austrialia? **P88**

Australia? **P26**

Or

Australea? **P1**

A land down under

As the mist clears, a dusty red landscape surrounds you. Scrubby trees with narrow leaves dot the countryside. It's hot and flies buzz around your face.

You swat a fly off your cheek. "Where are we?" you ask the sorcerer's apprentice.

"Crikey, ya wombat. Don't ya know?" Matilda says, rolling her eyes skyward. "We're in Australia! How good is that!"

Matilda is so happy, she's hopping around like it's Christmas morning.

You point off in the distance to a massive lump of red rock. "What's that?"

"Ayers rock," Matilda answers. "World's largest sandstone monolith. Over 1000 feet high and two miles long. She's a beauty eh?"

"It's pretty impressive," you say, "for a rock."

The sorcerer's apprentice chuckles. "If I'd known you were going to be so excited, Matilda, I'd have brought you here sooner."

"As long as we don't have to eat goanna," you say, screwing up your face. "Or kangaroo."

"Nothing wrong with barbecued roo," Matilda says.

You give her a doubtful look. "Let me guess. It tastes like chicken."

Matilda throws her head back and snorts. Then she gives you a withering look. "Jeez mate, you must be the world's only living brain donor! Tastes like chicken … ha! Now that's funny."

The sorcerer's apprentice brushes the flies away from his mouth before speaking. "Kangaroo taste a bit like beef and a bit like venison. Now crocodile — that tastes like chicken."

"Fishy chicken, to be exact," Matilda chimes in. "It's good with chips. Or, as you lot call them, French fries."

"Really? You've eaten crocodile?" Before your mouth closes again, a big fat blowfly lands on your tongue. "Pwwwaaa!" you spit. "Oh yuk. How do you put up with all these flies?"

"Just swallow them mate — good protein," Matilda says. "They taste like chicken!" This sets her off cackling like a crazy person. When she stops laughing, she shakes her head. "I'm joking — just keep your mouth shut when you're not talking. That'll help for a start."

"I hate to interrupt your talk about Australian cuisine, but you've got questions to answer. There's still a long way to go to get through the maze."

You point at the rock. "Can we go and climb it? The view from up there must be amazing." you say.

The apprentice shakes his head. "Ayers rock, or Uluru as the local Aborigines call it, is a sacred place. It would be disrespectful to climb it. But the sun will be setting soon. We could stay and watch the rock change color. It's a beautiful sight. Or, if you'd rather do something else, there's a special place I could take you."

"Where's that?" you ask.

"Now that would be telling. Don't you like surprises?"

It is time to make a decision. Do you:

Play it safe and watch the sunset? **P29**

Or

Take a chance and go for the surprise? **P49**

Stay and watch the sunset

"I like the idea of taking it easy and watching the rock change color," you say. "I've already had enough surprises for one day."

The apprentices nods slowly in understanding, then snaps his fingers. Three camp chairs appear. "We may as well be comfortable," he says.

You and Matilda sit and gaze towards the orange rock. It's shaped a bit like a huge loaf of bread with sloping ends. Eucalypts and stunted shrubs dot the flat land around it. As time passes and the sun lowers in the sky, the rock gets redder and redder. The light blue sky becomes darker and the horizon on either side of the rock becomes various shades of pink and lilac.

The rock is a hypnotic sight as the sound of the insects gradually fades.

Before you know it, the sun is gone and the sky is dark. Stars twinkle and the Milky Way runs across the sky like a vast river of light.

"Wow," you say. "I've never seen so many stars."

"It helps being over 200 miles away from the nearest town, and even Katherine isn't very big." the apprentice says. "No light pollution to spoil the view."

"She's a top spot," Matilda says. "But I'm getting hungry. Any chance of snapping up some tucker?"

"Tucker?" the apprentice asks, looking at you.

"Food," you translate.

You can see the apprentices white teeth glisten in the gloom. "I could probably rustle up some ice cream," he says.

"You beauty!" Matilda says.

The apprentice shoots you a glance.

"She likes the idea," you say. "I do too."

The apprentice chuckles. "But first—"

"—I'll need to answer a question," you interrupt.

"How did you guess?" The apprentice chuckles and reaches for his pocket. "If you get this right, you'll get a treat. But if you get it wrong, you might find yourself in the freezer yourself."

"In the freezer?" you ask. "That sounds uncomfortable."

The apprentice shrugs. "So is getting trampled by prehistoric animals."

Now you're really confused.

"Just ask the question, mate!" Matilda shouts. "Can't you see I'm hanging out for ice cream over here?"

"Okay, okay. Keep your hair on," the apprentice says.

"Not too hard please," you say. "I didn't pack a coat."

The apprentice unfolds a small piece of paper. "Okay, seeing this is a time-travel maze. How many seconds are there in one hour?"

Which is correct? Are there:

3,600 seconds in one hour? **P49**

Or

1400 seconds in one hour? **P96**

You have been sent to the future

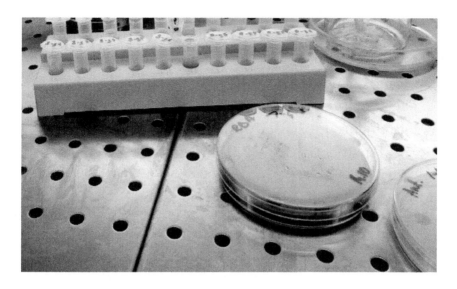

"Surprise!" the sorcerer's apprentice says. "Welcome to the future."

When the pink mist clears, you find yourself sitting at a long counter in a strange restaurant. Behind the counter, a stainless steel bench runs the length of the wall. In its centre is a gas grill. Beside the grill, a glass beaker filled with thick orange liquid bubbles in a Bunsen burner. The rest of the bench is covered in racks of test tubes, numerous glass beakers, funnels, and other equipment.

"They do good burgers here in 2040," the apprentice says. "The beef is grown in the lab. Very tender."

Matilda frowns. "But I don't want a hamburger grown in some Petri dish. That sounds gross!"

The cook behind the counter shakes her head and wipes

her hands on her apron. "It's exactly the same as the beef they sell in the shops, young lady."

"How can it be, when it doesn't even come from a cow?" Matilda asks, certain her teenage logic can't be faulted. "It's just some chemical cocktail you've mixed up in your lab."

The cook wags her finger at Matilda. "Stop being melodramatic. I'll have you know every cell that goes into my beef patties is cloned from the highest quality Angus beef."

"Cloned… Yuk!" Matilda says, twisting her face into a snarl.

The cook grabs a spatula from a long rack of utensils and puts half a dozen juicy patties on the grill. A cloud of steam billows up. The cook waves her hand through the steam guiding it towards her face and inhales deeply. She turns to the three of you. "You smell that and tell me it's not as good as store-bought."

Instead of smelling the rich aroma, Matilda pinches her nose and turns away.

"It smells good, Matilda," you say, grabbing at her arm. "Just like barbecue at home."

Matilda turns and glares at you. "You wouldn't know a decent barbie if one burned you on the backside."

You and the apprentice exchange glances.

The apprentice leans toward you. "What's got into her?" he whispers into your ear.

"She's just hungry I think," you say. "But she doesn't like anything that isn't natural."

"Well that's just silly," the apprentice says. "Just because it's natural doesn't mean it's good for you. Take hemlock or arsenic or uranium or lead or…"

"Yeah, yeah, I get the idea," you say. "But try to convince her of that. Believe me I've tried."

You look around the strange restaurant. There's a small centrifuge at one end of the bench where most restaurants would have a coffee machine. "Do they do milkshakes?" you ask.

The apprentice shakes his head. "Only soy. They don't milk cows any more. Too bad for the environment with all the methane they fart out."

Matilda sighs. "It's like being on the set of some sci-fi movie. Why can't we just go somewhere that has normal food?"

"But it's 2040," the sorcerer says, "this is normal. There are nearly 9 billion people to feed."

The cook laughs at Matilda's expression when she hears this, and then walks towards the fridge. She pulls two Petri dishes off the top shelf and places them on the counter beside three dinner plates. Then using long-handled tweezers, she removes some green leaves off a bed of pink agar. "You lot want lettuce on your burgers don't you?" she asks.

Matilda groans in horror as the cook carefully lays a crispy green leaf on what looks to be a whole meal bun.

"Well I'm game," you say. "I'm so hungry I'd eat just about anything."

Matilda grunts. "I'd rather starve than eat tha—that Franken-food."

The cook laughs. "It's just lettuce silly girl. I've cloned it from real plants. In fact it's healthier than farm-grown because I know there aren't any pesticides on it. And, it's fresh."

"Yeah, Matilda," the sorcerer's apprentice says. "Lettuce is lettuce, however it's grown. They only use the purest growing agar here."

Matilda scrunches up her face. "You can't call something fresh just because you've plucked it out of some Petri dish that's been festering in the fridge. That makes no sense."

The cook ignores Matilda and raises her eyebrows at you. "NaCl?"

"What?" you ask."

"NaCl? Do you want some?'

The apprentice sits in silence, a smirk on his face.

"Yuck, chemicals," Matilda mutters under her breath as she glares at the cook. "Has the world gone mad?"

"NaCl is salt silly," the cook says. "Absolutely everything is made up of chemicals. Now, do you want a sprinkle of sodium chloride on your burger or not?"

Matilda sighs and looks up towards the ceiling. "I … want …a …real … burger!"

"These are real," the cook says. "Rare, medium or well done?"

"Medium for me," the apprentice says.

"Me too," you agree, "with onions and mustard if you've

got it."

As the patties finish cooking, the cook moves along the bench to the beaker bubbling away above the blue and yellow flame.

Slipping on a heat-proof glove she lifts the beaker, holds it in front of her face, and swirls its contents. Satisfied the correct consistency has been achieved, she turns back to face the three of you. "Cheese sauce? It's vintage cheddar."

"Are you nuts?" Matilda howls. "That's not cheese!"

"Its chemical composition is exactly 100% cheese," the cook says. "I should know, I brewed it up this morning."

While Matilda sticks her finger down her throat and pretends to gag, you hear your stomach rumble. "Yes please," you say. "I love cheddar."

"In fact," the cook says stepping up to Matilda, "if I gave you my formula and what you call 'real' cheese, you couldn't tell the difference."

"I bet I could!" Matilda says.

The cook pours a small amount of her mixture into a spoon and passes it to Matilda. "Go on then. Taste it. Give me your honest opinion."

Matilda is reluctant at first. Then with a sigh she takes the spoon and smells. "I got to admit it smells like cheese."

"Go on. Taste it." the cook says.

Matilda lifts the spoon to her lips, squeezes her eyes closed and puts the spoon in her mouth. "Hmmm..." she says. "That's not bad."

"See, I told you. As long as the chemical composition is

the same, cheese is cheese no matter how you make it."

The cook lifts the beaker back to her nose and sniffs. "Perfect."

A girl about your age comes into the restaurant. She has long green hair and bangs. "Is that barbequed bovine I smell?"

The cook smiles. 'I'm making burgers for our visitors,' she says. "Want one?"

"Yes please," the girl says. "You make the best burgers in the whole universe."

"They're not real burgers," Matilda grumps. "She's grown the meat in her lab."

The cook gives the girl a smile "Don't listen to her, she doesn't understand how cloning works. She's from the past, poor girl."

The cook holds up the salt shaker. "Would you like some NaCl on your burger?"

"Yes please," the girl says. "It makes everything taste so much better."

"Okay, but just a little. Everything in moderation."

Matilda is back to sticking her finger down her throat and making retching noises.

"Stop that!" you say. "You're embarrassing me. Besides, it's rude."

Matilda grumbles, but does as she's asked.

"Let's grab a seat by the window so we can admire the view," the apprentice says.

You waste no time moving over to a table that looks out

over the city. Through light smog, you see a number of high-rise complexes, elevated transport thoroughfares, and hydroponic garden towers. Beyond the buildings, you catch a glimpse of the yellow-grey harbor, a faint chemical haze rising from its surface.

The newcomer comes over to your table. She seems to know the apprentice. "Hi," she says, "mind if I join you?"

"Sure," the apprentice says, pointing towards an empty chair. "These are my new friends."

As the girl sweeps a lock of green hair behind her right ear, you stare mesmerized at the large brown eye in the centre of her forehead. The girl smiles at you, and is about to says something when she catches a glimpse of her reflection in the glass.

"Oh no," she says, touching a small lump on her eyelid. "I've got a sty coming on."

"Don't worry," the cook says, placing a tray of burgers on the table. "I've genetically engineered this batch of lettuce to have antibiotic properties. Any infection should clear up in no time."

Matilda looks down at the burgers like she expecting them to grow legs and walk off. "Ewww!" she says, turning up her nose.

"I'll tell you what, Matilda," the sorcerer's apprentice says. "If you two answer the next question correctly, you can have some ice cream. How's that?"

Afraid the apprentice might send you off somewhere before you've eaten, you grab a burger and take a bite.

"Mmmmmm," you say, chewing like crazy. "These are great."

The girl with the one eye grabs one too, as does the apprentice.

Matilda crosses her arms for a moment, but then her hunger gets the better of her and she takes a burger too. "At least if I grow an eye in the middle of my head, I'll know what to blame." She bites in.

The girl laughs. "Burgers didn't make me this way. I'm from the far side of the solar system. My family travelled though a worm hole and arrived here a few years ago. We've been helping you humans clean up the mess you made of your planet. We're due to go home next week."

"Wow!" you say. "I noticed you were a little different, but I didn't want to be rude."

Matilda swallows. "Jeez, and I though Australia was a long way away."

The next few minutes are passed in silence as then four of you gobble down your food.

After wiping the juice off his chin, the apprentice pulls a small piece of paper out of his pocket. "Okay here's the next one. You ready?"

With a full stomach, you're ready for anything. You nod. "Do your worst."

The apprentice starts to read. "Right. What country sent the first man into space? Now be careful, you could end up anywhere."

It's time to make a decision:

Which statement is correct?

The first man in space was from the China. **P40**

The first man in space was from the U.S.S.R. **P44**

The first man in space was from the U.S.A. **P93**

China

When the pink mist clears, the sorcerer's apprentice is shaking his head. "Oops. I really thought you'd get that last one right."

You look around and see that you've been transported to the top of a massive stone wall. The wall runs along a mountainous ridge in both directions for as far as you can see. Watchtowers dot the wall every few miles.

"Is this what I think it is?" you ask the apprentice.

The apprentice shrugs. "Maybe. What are you thinking?"

"Is this the great wall of China?"

"How do you know about the great wall?" the apprentice asks.

"School," you reply. "I was once told that the Great Wall of China was the only manmade structure that was visible from space with the naked eye."

The apprentice chuckles. "Well whoever told you that obviously wasn't an astronaut. That's a common myth.

Astronauts can see city lights at night, but the wall, despite its size, is just too small to see without magnification of some sort." The apprentice points up the ridge towards one of the towers built into the wall. "Still, it's an impressive sight don't you think?"

"Let's check it out," Matilda says, heading up a series of shallow stone steps. "I want to get a photo from the top of that tower."

You glance over at the apprentice. "Are we allowed?"

"Okay but be careful," the apprentice says, taking off after Matilda. "This part of the wall is unmanned at the moment, but there could be northern tribesmen about."

"Northern tribesmen?" you ask as you climb the steps. Then you see the smirk on the apprentice's face. "Have you taken us back in time again?"

He nods. "I was wondering when you'd notice the lack of tourists. We're back at the time of the Ming dynasty."

"Ming? Like the famous pottery?" you ask.

"Yep, that's the one. The Chinese made lots of advances in ceramic manufacture from 1368 to 1644. They used to export it all over the world."

"Just like today," you say. "Only now they make all sorts of stuff."

Your comment gives the apprentice pause for thought. "Yeah, I suppose you're right."

The two of you head off in pursuit of Matilda. When you finally reach the base of the watchtower you find her sitting on the parapet, a low wall that runs along each side of the wall's top, designed to give troops protection from invaders, and to stop traders and their pack animals from falling over the edge. From this position, the full extent of the wall can be seen as it runs up and over hill after hill.

"Wow, this wall is bigger than I ever imagined," you say

Matilda seems unimpressed. "I'm hungry," she says. "It must be all this fresh air and exercise. Can you snap up some fried rice?"

The apprentice ignores your Australian friend and continues his history lesson. "They used these towers to watch out for the Mongol hoards, and would light fires or send other signals if danger was spotted. After 200 years or so, by the time all the different sections were built and joined up, the wall was about 5500 miles long and had 25,000 watchtowers."

"Wow," you say. "That's like Los Angeles to New York."

"And back," the apprentice says. "LA to New York is only 2,400 miles."

"Crikey," Matilda says, "and to think they did it all by hand."

"Yep," the apprentice says, "millions of men over hundreds of years."

"This is all very interesting," you say, "but how are we going to get home from here?"

The apprentice reaches for his pocket. "How about I ask you another question. Maybe you'll get it right this time?"

You think a moment. "Okay," you say with a shrug. "What have I got to lose?"

The apprentice reads what's on the paper in front of him. "Here we go. What is the capital of China? If you get this right we'll go and have some ice cream.

You see Matilda's eyes light up.

"But if you get it wrong," the apprentice says, giving you a serious look. "I'll have to spin the dial on the time machine and who knows where we'll end up."

It is time to make a decision.

Is the capital of China:

Beijing? **P49**

Or

Tokyo? **P44**

Red Square

"Where are we now?" you ask, rubbing your temples as the mist clears. "This time travelling is giving me a headache."

Matilda hugs herself and shivers. "Well it's not tropical northern Australia. That's for sure."

"It's not Tokyo either," you say, looking around.

The sky is cloudy and the air is cold. You are standing in the middle of a huge cobblestoned plaza. The buildings around it are like nothing you've ever seen. Have you been transported into a fairytale?

The largest building has towering bricked walls topped with striped turrets shaped like upside-down onions. One turret has spiraling blue and white stripes. Another has a cross-hatch of red and green. One has stripes of green and gold — and there are more. The top turret looks like it's made from solid gold as it shimmers in the light.

You look around for the apprentice and find him standing behind you. He is wearing a long overcoat and a fur cap. "Welcome to Red Square," he says.

"Where's that?" Matilda asks.

"In Moscow," he says, "the capital of Russia. So what do you think of St. Basil's Cathedral?"

"The one with the turrets?" you ask.

The apprentice nods. "Beautiful isn't it."

"Why did you bring us here?" you ask. "Are you trying to get us arrested as spies by the KGB?"

The apprentice chuckles and shakes his head. "It's only 1861. The cathedral's just been completed. The KGB doesn't even exist yet."

"Jeez," Matilda says. "We'll never get home at this rate."

The apprentice ignores Matilda's whining. "A few apprentices have been Russian you know. One was even close to the royal family. Ever heard of Rasputin? He was a confidant of Nicholas II, the last tsar. "

"I've heard of Rasputin! Was he really a sorcerer's apprentice?" you ask.

"Not a very good one, unfortunately," the apprentice says. "He caused quite an uproar in his day."

"What did he do wrong?" Matilda asks.

"Rather than finishing the maze like he was supposed to, he decided to stop answering questions and become a wandering mystic. Broke all the rules. Got poor Nicholas in all sorts of trouble. But we don't have time for a Russian history lesson. You'll have to Google him when you get back home."

"If we get back," Matilda says, stomping her feet to stay warm. "Assuming I don't die from cold or hunger first!"

SNAP!

Suddenly you and Matilda are wearing fur hats and long coats like the apprentice.

Matilda smiles, "Great coat! Now, how about rustling up some ice cream?"

The apprentice frowns. "You never stop trying do you?"

"I didn't get where I am today without trying," she says, standing a little taller and looking rather pleased with herself.

"What are you talking about? You're in Russia!" you yell at her. "It's winter and it's freezing! You sent us back in time!" You shake your head in amazement. "...I didn't get where I am today... Jeez, Matilda, what's wrong with you?"

"Nothing a large bowl of ice cream wouldn't fix," she says, with a smirk. "Relax. The sorcerer's apprentice here has got everything under control."

"Grrrrr..." You turn away and stomp off across the square.

"Hey where are you going?" the apprentice yells out after you. "You need to answer the next question!"

"Rasputin didn't!" you say without turning around.

Let 'em sweat, you think. Surely the apprentice isn't allowed to lose you while you're in the maze. Maybe you'll go have a look at the cathedral.

SNAP!

You are instantly back beside the apprentice. "Stay put and do as you're told," he growls. "One Rasputin in history is enough. Now, answer this next question and you'll move closer to home."

"Or get ice cream," Matilda says glancing towards the apprentice. "That's a possibility too isn't it? I'm sure I heard you mention ice cream."

The apprentice sighs and stares back at Matilda. "If I say having ice cream is a possibility will you shut up for a few minutes?"

Matilda mimes zipping her mouth shut.

"Okay…" the apprentice says reluctantly. "It's a possibility … a faint one. Happy now?"

Matilda smiles, and then turns to you. "See? I told ya that Persistence is my middle name."

"But get the question wrong and I'll send you further back," the apprentice says. "Would you like that? Miss Persistence?"

"Like a poke in the eye with a burnt stick," Matilda says.

"Translation?" the apprentice says, turning to you.

"She wouldn't be happy."

The apprentice scratches his head. "Right, hmmm…"

Matilda stomps her foot. "Well don't keep us in suspenders, Mister apprentice. Read out the question. I'm starving in case you'd forgotten."

"Matilda! Stop being a pain in the butt," you say.

"No pain, no gain," she replies.

"I don't think that's what that saying means," you say.

"It does in Australia," she insists. "When I'm a pain, I get gain."

"No wonder they sent you overseas to school," you say, before turning towards the apprentice. "You may as well get it over with, but please don't ask me about Russia. All I know about Russia is that it's the largest country in the world. Followed by Canada and the United States."

The apprentice nods and reaches for his pocket. "Ah… Here's a good one. You should get this."

"You'd better!" Matilda says glaring at you for a moment. Then she smiles. "Just joking. No pressure."

"Right," the apprentice says. "What is the most accurate clock in the world? Is it:"

A grandfather clock? **P78**

Or

An atomic clock? **P83**

Welcome to the sorcerer's ice cream parlor

When the mist clears, you find yourself in a large ice cream parlor with a long counter and lots of tables. The place echoes with groups eating and laughing. The apprentice is dressed like a clown in a bright blue jumpsuit with yellow dots and floppy red shoes.

"Well done. Time for ice cream," he says, with a grin.

"Yippee!" Matilda cries. "Nom, nom, nom!"

The apprentice taps one of his over-sized shoes on the floor. "Okay, what's your favorite flavor? Quick now, before the sorcerer changes his mind."

"Kangaroo," Matilda says with a laugh. "Skippy if you've got it."

The sorcerer's apprentice gives Matilda a confused looked. "I—I'm not sure the sorcerer does kangaroo ice—"

"Ha! Gottcha!" Matilda shouts. "Jeez mate, for a sorcerer's apprentice you're awfully gullible. Nah, seriously, I'll have passion fruit if you've got it."

The apprentice swivels around. "And you?"

"Chocolate, please." you say, "with chocolate chips, chocolate sprinkles and chocolate sauce."

"Right," the apprentice says. "One kangaroo and one vanilla coming up."

As the apprentice goes to the counter, you and Matilda find a seat.

"I wonder who all these people are?" Matilda asks. "Do you reckon they're on trips through the maze too?"

You study the groups. "They could be. Did you notice every table has one person dressed like a clown?

Matilda scans the room. "You're right, there's a whole circus of them."

"Here we go," the sorcerer's apprentice says placing a bowl in front of each of you. "Now eat."

"Strewth mate! What the bleedin' heck you call this? There's hair and—and, all sorts of stuff in mine."

"Who the gullible one now?" the apprentice says, giving Matilda a wink. "You really think the sorcerer can't make kangaroo ice cream?"

"Ewww," Matilda says, shoving the bowl away. "I need this like a submarine needs a screen door."

"Translation?" the apprentice says, looking at you.

"She's not happy," you say with a chuckle.

Matilda harrumphs. "Would you be? Jeez, bloke can't

even take a joke."

The apprentice takes a bite of his ice cream and lets Matilda stew. Then, he snaps his fingers over her bowl, and in a puff of sweet-smelling smoke, her kangaroo ice cream transforms into passion fruit, topped with a juicy pulp filled with tiny black seeds.

"Now that's more like it!" Matilda shouts. She grabs a spoon and digs in. "Neat trick."

"The sorcerer teaches all of his apprentices magic. You'd be surprised what I can do."

Matilda swallows a big mouthful. "How did you become an apprentice?"

"Anyone can do it. I'll tell you at the end of the maze. If you get there," he says. "In the meantime, finish your ice cream. You've got more questions to answer."

"So are all these clowns apprentices?" you ask.

The boy nods as he shovels ice cream into his mouth.

You do some quick calculations. "But there must be 50 of them."

The boy swallows. "The sorcerer needs lot of apprentices to show visitors through his mazes and to help with all the questions. Your next question was made up by a boy named Luke."

You and Matilda scoop up the last of your ice cream as the apprentice pulls a piece of paper out of his pocket. "Okay, here we go. Get this right and we'll go someplace fun. Get it wrong and you might wish you were wearing something warmer."

"You're not going to stuff us in the freezer with the ice cream are you?" Matilda asks.

The apprentice shakes his head. "Not quite," he says. "Right, here's your question. At what temperature is Fahrenheit and Celsius the same?"

It is time for your decision.

Is it:

Zero degrees? **P53**

Or

Minus 40 degrees? **P57**

You have chosen zero degrees

"Oops, that's not right," the sorcerer's apprentice says. "Looks like I'll have to spin the dial and see where we end up. Hold on!"

FLASH—BANG!

This time the mist is blue and cold. As it clears, the freezing cloud sinks to the ground, but doesn't disappear altogether. When you look around, you find yourself standing on the bank of a river. The water rushing past is light blue in color because of the flecks of ice suspended in it. Further upstream, about half a mile or so, is a huge wall of ice with pointed pinnacles. Icebergs float in the water at the foot of the ice.

A bitter wind blows down the valley, rustling your hair and chilling your ears. Goose bumps pop up on your arm.

"Whoa!" Matilda says. "Is that a glacier up there?"

"Good guess," the sorcerer's apprentice says.

"It's free—freezing," you say between chattering teeth. "Any cha—chance of a quick question before I get hypothermia?"

The apprentice snaps his fingers and a long hairy robe appears over your shoulders. It smells a bit rank, but it cuts the wind and stops your teeth from chattering. Matilda has been transformed into a cave girl in her roughly-fashioned wrap.

You pluck at your garment. "By the looks of the clothing you've given us, I'm guessing we've gone back in time again?"

"Well spotted," the apprentice says. "We've gone back to the last ice age 14,000 years ago."

But Matilda isn't listening. Her face is screwed into an expression of disgust as she picks at something in her coat "This thing smells like wombat pee," she complains, pinching her nose between her thumb and forefinger. "If it weren't so cold…"

"They cured animal skins with urine back then," the apprentice says. "Pee's got ammonia in it. Sorry if you're not happy."

"Too right I'm not happy," Matilda says. "It's got fleas too."

The apprentice snaps his finger and dozens of small insects fall like pepper onto the snow at Matilda's feet. "There you go," he says, "no more fleas."

"But the smell…" she says.

SNAP! A strawberry cloud surrounds Matilda.

"Now, can we get on with it?" the apprentice says, giving Matilda a sharp look.

"Yeah, thanks," Matilda says. She licks her lips. "That's much better."

"So what's next?" you ask. "Are you going to question us about the Ice Age?"

The apprentice is about to answer when a sharp crack breaks the silence. Further up the valley, a pillar of the ice the size of a 10 story building shears off the glacier. With a huge splash, the ice crashes into the water at the glacier's base. A thirty-foot wave rushes down the river towards you.

"Quick! Get to higher ground!" the apprentice shouts, before turning and running up the slope.

You quickly follow as the wave roars down the valley picking up rocks and other debris as it goes. Matilda is right beside you pumping her arms furiously as she rushes up the hill.

"Up here," the apprentice says, scrambling up a gravel slope between two huge boulders.

You don't need to look back to tell the wave is closing. The rumbling is right behind you. Just as you reach the top, the water rushes past, only yards below.

You lie on the ground, panting.

"Crikey, tha—that was close!" Matilda says, gasping for air. "Thought we were goners."

Your hands are shaking, and it's not from the cold. "Can

we leave now?" you ask the apprentice. "Getting killed wasn't on my 'to do' list today.

"Good idea," he says, pulling a piece of paper from his pocket. "The sorcerer would be pretty annoyed if I lost you mid-maze." He tucks the time machine under his arm and reads from the paper. "The glaciers are shrinking. In fact we're standing on a pile of rock that the glacier pushed down the mountain before it retreated. What is this pile of rock called?"

"I think I know this one!" Matilda says. "Please can I answer it?"

But you think you know the answer too. What should you do?

It is time to make your next decision. Is the pile of rock called:

A glacial moraine? **P62**

Or

A glacial meringue? **P85**

Or

Do you let Matilda answer the question? **P83**

You have chosen minus 40 degrees

"Well done," the apprentice says.

You give him a smile. "Yeah, well I knew that 0 degrees was freezing in Celsius and 32 was freezing in Fahrenheit so it had to be the other choice."

"Nice logic," the apprentice says. "You used what is known as 'the process of elimination' to work it out. You eliminated a wrong answer and it left you with the correct one."

"Whatever," Matilda says with a sigh. "Are you going to get us closer to home, or are you two going to stand around and chinwag all day?"

"Be patient," the apprentice says. "I just need to decide where I should take you."

"Somewhere warm," you suggest. "All this talk of freezing has made me nervous."

The apprentice scratches his head, then smiles. "I have an idea…" He holds up the box and turns the dial.

You stick your fingers in your ears. The coil glows red. The air crackles.

FLASH–BANG!

"Crikey that was loud," Matilda says as the mist clears. "My ears are ringing."

White sand and coconut palms edge a crystal clear ocean like pictures you've seen on postcards. The water is calm, with barely a ripple on its surface. Gulls dip and dive.

The apprentice is submerged up to his chest. "Come on

in," he yells, "the water's fantastic!"

The sun blazes down. Grains of sand squeak between your toes. You certainly got your wish for somewhere warm.

"Last one in is a wombat's bum!" Matilda shrieks as she dashes for the sea.

You take off after her. By the time she reaches the water's edge, the two of you are side by side. You plough through the shallows until the water is thigh deep then plunge forward arching into a shallow dive. But when you surface and look around, the apprentice is nowhere to be seen.

"Where'd he go?" Matilda says, searching for the boy. "I hope that cheeky sod hasn't deserted us."

"He's probably diving for shells. He wouldn't leave without us would he?"

"Blowed if I know, mate."

"Well I'm going for a swim," you say before paddling out a little further. "Look how clear the water is."

Then your stomach lurches. A grey fin is cutting though the water further out. "Umm… Matilda…" You raise an arm and point at the triangle as it turns in a gentle arc, heading closer. "Is that what I think it is?"

"Bleedin' heck!" Matilda says. She turns and thrashes her way towards the shore. "I'm not sure what it is," she says over her shoulder, "but I'm not hangin' round to find out."

A second fin pops out of the water, and a third. Before you've had a chance to react, they streak towards you. A shadow moves under the water right beside you.

"Ahhhhhhhhhhhh!" you scream.

When the apprentice surfaces, there is a huge grin on his face. "Fancy a dolphin ride?" he says. "Oh, sorry… Did I give you a fright?"

"Give me a fright!" you shout. "I thought you were a shark! I nearly pooped myself!"

You hear cackling from the beach. When you turn towards shore, Matilda is standing in ankle-deep water, clutching at her sides, laughing.

"You should have seen your face." she says, pointing at you. "I didn't realize human eyes could bug out like that."

"Sorry," the boy said. "I thought you knew the difference between dolphins and sharks."

"Obviously not!" you snap, wishing your heart would stop banging so hard in your chest.

"Well for future reference, the back of a sharks fin is pretty straight up and down. Dolphin dorsal fins are more curved."

"Might pay to tell that to your guests a little earlier next time," you say. "Save on laundry."

But your fright goes away when the dolphins surface beside the boy. They have smiley faces and sparkling eyes. He strokes one of the dolphins under its chin.

Another rubs its narrow snout against your arm to get your attention.

"I think they want to play," the apprentice says. He lifts one leg over a dolphin's back and grabbing gently onto its dorsal fin. "Climb on. It's like riding a horse, only wetter."

A dolphin nudges you again, so you do as the apprentice

suggests and climb on.

The dolphin's skin is smooth and has a slightly rubbery texture to it, almost like the creature is wearing a wet suit. Sitting on its back, you feel warmth radiate from its body. The dolphin makes a series of squeaky clicks then starts to swim after the apprentice.

"Oi! Wait for me you lot!" Matilda yells, splashing back into the water. "Here dolphin, come to Matilda."

As if understanding her words, the last dolphin streaks over to Matilda and allows her to climb onto its back.

"Where are they taking us?" you ask the apprentice as the dolphins move into formation, three abreast. You point to a speck of land in the distance. "Are we going to that island?"

The island looks to be about a mile offshore. It's small and only has a few palm trees on it.

"We're going to visit the sea turtles," the apprentice says. "The island is part of Ulithi atoll, one of their most important nesting sites."

The dolphins' tails are powerful as they move up and down, propelling the three of you though the water. As you near the beach, the water becomes shallower and bright corals and schools of small, colorful fish appear beneath you.

The sea around you is busy with life. Urchins, anemones, starfish and crabs clutter the bottom, while fish swim in groups. They jink left, then right, searching for food amongst the coral and avoiding the larger fish who'd like them for lunch.

Then you see your first turtle. Its carapace, or shell, is a brownish-green and is at least a yard wide.

"Wow they're so big!" you say. "I expected them to be smaller."

"Adults can grow to over 600 pounds," the apprentice says.

"That's a lot of turtle soup," Matilda says. "Not that I'm suggesting—"

"—you'd better not be," the apprentice says a little sharply, "they're endangered. Now, the next question is about turtles, so listen carefully." The apprentice climbs off his dolphin and walks up onto the beach.

You and Matilda follow.

"Mother turtles crawl up the beach and dig a hole in the sand with their back flippers," the apprentice says. "Then they lay their eggs before covering them up. After two months, when the baby turtles hatch, they're only a couple of inches long."

"How many eggs do they lay?" you ask.

"Ah… I see you've stumbled upon my next question. How many eggs *do* they lay? Now if you get this right, you'll nearly be home. But if you get this one wrong, I'll have to send you back in time. So, which statement is correct?"

Green sea turtles lay between 10 and 20 eggs in each nest. **P79**

Or

Green sea turtles lay between 100 and 200 eggs in each nest. **P83**

You have been sent to the future

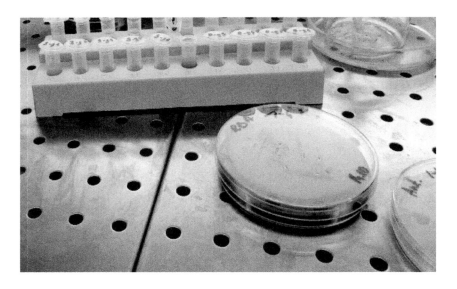

"Surprise!" the sorcerer's apprentice says. "Welcome to the future."

When the pink mist clears, you find yourself sitting at a long counter in a strange restaurant. Behind the counter, a stainless steel bench runs the length of the wall. In its centre is a gas grill. Beside the grill, a glass beaker filled with thick orange liquid bubbles in a Bunsen burner. The rest of the bench is covered in racks of test tubes, numerous glass beakers, funnels, and other equipment.

"They do good burgers here in 2040," the apprentice says. "The beef is grown in the lab. Very tender."

Matilda frowns. "But I don't want a hamburger grown in some Petri dish. That sounds gross!"

The cook behind the counter shakes her head and wipes

her hands on her apron. "It's exactly the same as the beef they sell in the shops, young lady."

"How can it be, when it doesn't even come from a cow?" Matilda asks, certain her teenage logic can't be faulted. "It's just some chemical cocktail you've mixed up in your lab."

The cook wags her finger at Matilda. "Stop being melodramatic. I'll have you know every cell that goes into my beef patties is cloned from the highest quality Angus beef."

"Cloned… Yuk!" Matilda says, twisting her face into a snarl.

The cook grabs a spatula from a long rack of utensils and puts half a dozen juicy patties on the grill. A cloud of steam billows up. The cook waves her hand through the steam guiding it towards her face and inhales deeply. She turns to the three of you. "You smell that and tell me it's not as good as store-bought."

Instead of smelling the rich aroma, Matilda pinches her nose and turns away.

"It smells good, Matilda," you say, grabbing at her arm. "Just like barbecue at home."

Matilda turns and glares at you. "You wouldn't know a decent barbie if one burned you on the backside."

You and the apprentice exchange glances.

The apprentice leans toward you. "What's got into her?" he whispers into your ear.

"She's just hungry I think," you say. "But she doesn't like anything that isn't natural."

"Well that's just silly," the apprentice says. "Just because it's natural doesn't mean it's good for you. Take hemlock or arsenic or uranium or lead or…"

"Yeah, yeah, I get the idea," you say. "But try to convince her of that. Believe me I've tried."

You look around the strange restaurant. There's a small centrifuge at one end of the bench where most restaurants would have a coffee machine. "Do they do milkshakes?" you ask.

The apprentice shakes his head. "Only soy. They don't milk cows any more. Too bad for the environment with all the methane they fart out."

Matilda sighs. "It's like being on the set of some sci-fi movie. Why can't we just go somewhere that has normal food?"

"But it's 2040," the sorcerer says, "this is normal. There are nearly 9 billion people to feed."

The cook laughs at Matilda's expression when she hears this, and then walks towards the fridge. She pulls two Petri dishes off the top shelf and places them on the counter beside three dinner plates. Then using long-handled tweezers, she removes some green leaves off a bed of pink agar. "You lot want lettuce on your burgers don't you?" she asks.

Matilda groans in horror as the cook carefully lays a crispy green leaf on what looks to be a whole meal bun.

"Well I'm game," you say. "I'm so hungry I'd eat just about anything."

Matilda grunts. "I'd rather starve than eat tha—that Franken-food."

The cook laughs. "It's just lettuce silly girl. I've cloned it from real plants. In fact it's healthier than farm-grown because I know there aren't any pesticides on it. And, it's fresh."

"Yeah, Matilda," the sorcerer's apprentice says. "Lettuce is lettuce, however it's grown. They only use the purest growing agar here."

Matilda scrunches up her face. "You can't call something fresh just because you've plucked it out of some Petri dish that's been festering in the fridge. That makes no sense."

The cook ignores Matilda and raises her eyebrows at you. "NaCl?"

"What?" you ask."

"NaCl? Do you want some?'

The apprentice sits in silence, a smirk on his face.

"Yuck, chemicals," Matilda mutters under her breath as she glares at the cook. "Has the world gone mad?"

"NaCl is salt silly," the cook says. "Absolutely everything is made up of chemicals. Now, do you want a sprinkle of sodium chloride on your burger or not?"

Matilda sighs and looks up towards the ceiling. "I … want …a …real … burger!"

"These are real," the cook says. "Rare, medium or well done?"

"Medium for me," the apprentice says.

"Me too," you agree, "with onions and mustard if you've

got it."

As the patties finish cooking, the cook moves along the bench to the beaker bubbling away above the blue and yellow flame.

Slipping on a heat-proof glove she lifts the beaker, holds it in front of her face, and swirls its contents. Satisfied the correct consistency has been achieved, she turns back to face the three of you. "Cheese sauce? It's vintage cheddar."

"Are you nuts?" Matilda howls. "That's not cheese!"

"Its chemical composition is exactly 100% cheese," the cook says. "I should know, I brewed it up this morning."

While Matilda sticks her finger down her throat and pretends to gag, you hear your stomach rumble. "Yes please," you say. "I love cheddar."

"In fact," the cook says stepping up to Matilda, "if I gave you my formula and what you call 'real' cheese, you couldn't tell the difference."

"I bet I could!" Matilda says.

The cook pours a small amount of her mixture into a spoon and passes it to Matilda. "Go on then. Taste it. Give me your honest opinion."

Matilda is reluctant at first. Then with a sigh she takes the spoon and smells. "I got to admit it smells like cheese."

"Go on. Taste it." the cook says.

Matilda lifts the spoon to her lips, squeezes her eyes closed and puts the spoon in her mouth. "Hmmm…" she says. "That's not bad."

"See, I told you. As long as the chemical composition is

the same, cheese is cheese no matter how you make it."

The cook lifts the beaker back to her nose and sniffs. "Perfect."

A girl about your age comes into the restaurant. She has long green hair and bangs. "Is that barbequed bovine I smell?"

The cook smiles. 'I'm making burgers for our visitors,' she says. "Want one?"

"Yes please," the girl says. "You make the best burgers in the whole universe."

"They're not real burgers," Matilda grumps. "She's grown the meat in her lab."

The cook gives the girl a smile "Don't listen to her, she doesn't understand how cloning works. She's from the past, poor girl."

The cook holds up the salt shaker. "Would you like some NaCl on your burger?"

"Yes please," the girl says. "It makes everything taste so much better."

"Okay, but just a little. Everything in moderation."

Matilda is back to sticking her finger down her throat and making retching noises.

"Stop that!" you say. "You're embarrassing me. Besides, it's rude."

Matilda grumbles, but does as she's asked.

"Let's grab a seat by the window so we can admire the view," the apprentice says.

You waste no time moving over to a table that looks out

over the city. Through light smog, you see a number of high-rise complexes, elevated transport thoroughfares, and hydroponic garden towers. Beyond the buildings, you catch a glimpse of the yellow-grey harbor, a faint chemical haze rising from its surface.

The newcomer comes over to your table. She seems to know the apprentice. "Hi," she says, "mind if I join you?"

"Sure," the apprentice says, pointing towards an empty chair. "These are my new friends."

As the girl sweeps a lock of green hair behind her right ear, you stare mesmerized at the large brown eye in the centre of her forehead. The girl smiles at you, and is about to says something when she catches a glimpse of her reflection in the glass.

"Oh no," she says, touching a small lump on her eyelid. "I've got a sty coming on."

"Don't worry," the cook says, placing a tray of burgers on the table. "I've genetically engineered this batch of lettuce to have antibiotic properties. Any infection should clear up in no time."

Matilda looks down at the burgers like she expecting them to grow legs and walk off. "Ewww!" she says, turning up her nose.

"I'll tell you what, Matilda," the sorcerer's apprentice says. "If you two answer the next question correctly, you can have some ice cream. How's that?"

Afraid the apprentice might send you off somewhere before you've eaten, you grab a burger and take a bite.

"Mmmmmm," you say, chewing like crazy. "These are great."

The girl with the one eye grabs one too, as does the apprentice.

Matilda crosses her arms for a moment, but then her hunger gets the better of her and she takes a burger too. "At least if I grow an eye in the middle of my head, I'll know what to blame." She bites in.

The girl laughs. "Burgers didn't make me this way. I'm from the far side of the solar system. My family travelled though a worm hole and arrived here a few years ago. We've been helping you humans clean up the mess you made of your planet. We're due to go home next week."

"Wow!" you say. "I noticed you were a little different, but I didn't want to be rude."

Matilda swallows. "Jeez, and I though Australia was a long way away."

The next few minutes are passed in silence as then four of you gobble down your food.

After wiping the juice off his chin, the apprentice pulls a small piece of paper out of his pocket. "Okay here's the next one. You ready?"

With a full stomach, you're ready for anything. You nod. "Do your worst."

The apprentice starts to read. "Right. What country sent the first man into space? Now be careful, because one of these answers will send you back to the very beginning of the maze."

70

It's time to make a decision:
Which statement is correct?
The first man in space was from the China. **P40**
The first man in space was from the U.S.S.R. **P44**
The first man in space was from the U.S.A. **P88**

Glacial moraine

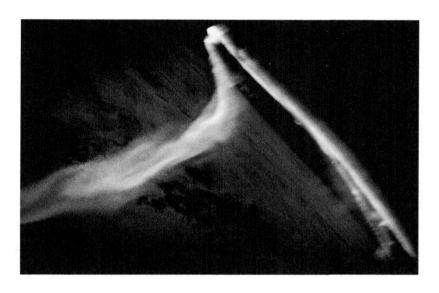

FLASH—BANG!

"That's rightttttttttttt," the apprentice says, his voice fading away.

You are falling down an endless tunnel. Colors swirl and static crackles all around you. What's going on? This isn't what usually happens when you travel through space-time. Have you fallen into a worm hole? Are you being sucked into an alternative universe? Did Matilda cause this somehow?

You grit your teeth and squint to protect your eyes from the bursts of bright green, vivid blues, purples and hot pink light that twists and dances before you. It is all so strange.

Matilda streaks past you in a swirl of color. "Crikeyyyyyyyyyyyyy!"

Where is she going? What is going on? "Matilda!" you yell.

Then, as fast as your falling started, you find yourself hovering above the horizon. The curve of the earth stretches out before you. Green lights flash and spread out. Waves dance and swirl, constantly changing as they flicker like flames across the sky.

"Streuth! That was different."

You turn to find Matilda floating beside you in a white space suit. The helmet's faceplate is made from clear plastic and you can see her startled expression clearly through it. In all the excitement, you hadn't noticed that you have a suit on too.

"What do you think of the aurora borealis?" say the apprentice.

You look around but he is nowhere to be seen.

"Beautiful isn't it?" the apprentice says.

His voice is coming directly into your helmet. Then you see him in the distance. He's floating towards you, adjusting his course as he does so with tiny jets of compressed air shooting from the pack attached to his back.

"What's going on? For a moment I thought we were falling through a worm hole." you say, looking down at the dancing lights.

The apprentice shakes his helmet. "Not quite. Pretty amazing show, don't you think?"

"What causes all the lights?" you ask.

"It happens when charged particles from the sun hit

electrons in our atmosphere."

As you watch the lights dance, your mind is taken off the fact that you're floating in space.

"I think I'm more worried about getting back to earth in one piece," Matilda says, breaking the spell "Haven't you forgotten something?"

The apprentice does a quick scan of the area, then looks back at Matilda. "Not that I can see…"

Matilda sighs in frustration and glares at the boy. "Like a bleedin' spaceship, you great galah!"

"Oh that," the apprentice chuckles. "Don't worry. I have a plan." He pulls the black box from a pouch on his right leg and starts fiddling with the dial. "Right, I've adjusted the time slightly, the space taxi should be along at any moment."

"Space taxi?" you say. "Are you serious?"

"Well, officially its call the International Space Station, but we should be able to cadge a lift if we ask nicely."

"Ha!" Matilda scoffs. "Ask nicely? That's your plan?"

"Seems to work for most things I've found," the apprentice says. "Oh here it comes, right on schedule. Clip on to my tether, I'll maneuver us over."

After you and Matilda are attached, the apprentice gives his jets a couple of long bursts so you match speed with the space station. Then with one final burst he brings you alongside the glistening craft.

"Grab hold and don't let go," the apprentice says, grabbing a handrail. "I'll send them a message and get them to open the air lock."

Matilda taps you on the shoulder. "I hope this wombat knows what he's doing."

"I can hear you Matilda!" the apprentice says. "ISS, this is the sorcerer's apprentice, we're just outside. Can we come aboard please?"

"This is the ISS. Please make your way to the airlock."

"Come on you two," the apprentice says, "time to make our grand entry."

The three of you work your way along the handrail to a door built into the side of the space station.

"Airlock, disengaged," a voice says in your helmet.

And with that, the door pops open, exposing an area the size of an elevator.

"Right, in we get," the apprentices says.

Once the three of you are inside, the apprentice pushes a button on the wall and the door closes with a hiss. A dial starts to move from red to green as the atmosphere inside the airlock is equalized with the main ship.

"Okay we can take off our suits now," the apprentice says. The inner door opens revealing a man wearing blue overalls. "Here let me help you with those."

The apprentice grins. "What do you think? Quite a place eh?"

Once the suits are stowed in lockers, the man leads you down a narrow corridor lined with pipes and other equipment. Everywhere you look are dials and ducts and wiring and control panels. Once through the corridor the space opens out, but it is still cluttered with equipment, microscopes, and other electronics. There are also three more people waiting to meet you, a man and a woman, also wearing blue, and a man with a Chinese flag on his suit.

The man in blue floats over to you and gives you all a puzzled look. "This is the first time we've picked up hitchhikers. I'm the captain of this mission. Do you mind telling me how the heck you got here?"

The apprentice smiles. "I'm guiding my friends through a space-time maze." He pulls out the black box. "Neat gadget, eh?"

The captain's face creases in confusion. "You got here with that—that box? But that's—"

"—impossible?" The apprentice shrugs. "How do you explain us being here then?"

The captain continues. "Hmmmm. Yes you have a point... So, how does it work?"

The apprentice smiles. "Well if I knew that, I'd be the sorcerer and not his apprentice, wouldn't I?"

"The sorcerer?" the captain says. "You mean you got here by magic?"

The apprentice nods. "If you call this box magic, then I guess we did. The sorcerer is a scientist that works at the Timescale Research Facility. This is his invention. I'm just running some field trials for him. It only seems like magic to those of us who can't explain it. To the sorcerer it's no more complicated than a microwave oven or a cell phone."

"Field trials? And you ended up here on the International Space Station? I'll have to contact Houston. They're going to flip when they hear about this."

The sorcerer's apprentice snaps his fingers.

FLASH—BANG!

The room filled with pink mist. When the mist clears you are sitting in a quiet waiting room. Matilda is to your right. You turn and face the apprentice. "What was that all about? And where are we now? Are we back on earth?"

"Yes, we had to go. Those astronauts were getting a bit nosey. So I brought us back to the sorcerer's place."

"But won't they want to know where we've gone?"

The apprentice grins. "Don't worry they won't remember a thing. The mist I left behind will see to that."

"You've given them amnesia?" Matilda says.

"I had to. We can't have people reporting they've seen time travelers. The authorities will think they're crazy and lock them up. That wouldn't be very nice of us now would it?"

Matilda laughs. "You're full of tricks aren't you?"

"Yep," the apprentice says. "That's what being a sorcerer's apprentice is all about."

"So this is the sorcerer's place?" you ask.

"Well actually it's the sorcerer's waiting room," the apprentice says. "Wait here, I'll go into his office and see if he's ready to see you yet."

With that, the boy snaps his fingers and disappears.

You give Matilda a look. "I wonder if this is the end of the maze then."

"Let's hope so," she says. "I'm famished."

A few minutes later, a booming voice comes over the intercom.

"It is time for another question," the voice rumbles.

"Crikey, that must be the sorcerer," Matilda says.

"If you get the question right, you will get to return home," the voice continues. "But if you get it wrong, I will send you back in time. So listen carefully."

"Which of the following statements is correct?"

The International Space Station orbits the earth every 90 minutes. **P83**

Or

The International Space Station orbits the earth once a day. **P78**

Back in time

"It's dark," Matilda says. "Where are we?"

"I think we're in a cave," you reply.

Standing quietly as your eyes adjust, you listen to the sounds around you. Somewhere further into the cave you hear the steady *plonk, plonk, plonk* of water dripping.

After a minute or so, you start to see shadows. A small amount of light is seeping into the cave through a crack high in the rock above you. Wisps of smoke drift up from the remnants of a fire inside a semicircle of rocks built up against one wall.

"Someone's been down here," you say. "And they haven't been gone very long by the looks of those ashes."

"Where's the apprentice?" Matilda asks, looking around nervously. "I hope he's not too far, it's chilly down here and

I'm a bit claustrophobic."

Next to the makeshift fireplace is a pile of branches. You kneel down on the ground and blow on the embers. A couple pieces glow red.

"I'll see if I can get this fire going," you say. "It'll warm us up and give us some light while we figure out what to do."

You grab one of the smaller branches and break it into pieces. These you lay gently over the embers.

"Don't smother it, mate," Matilda says. "It needs air to burn."

You purse you lips and blow. The extra oxygen makes the embers glow red-hot and before you know it, the small pile of kindling bursts into flames. Slowly, you add more twigs and branches to the growing fire.

It isn't until you look up from your task that you spot the paintings on the wall behind you.

"Whoa!" you say taking in the scene. "Matilda, look behind you!"

Matilda turns. Her eyes widen. "That's amazing!"

Matilda isn't exaggerating. The back wall of the cave, opposite the fire, is covered in simple, yet beautiful paintings. Images of deer, horses and other grazing animals stretch from one side of the cave to the other. One animal looks a bit like a giraffe. In the centre of the wall is a painting of a fire, not unlike your own. Around it, the artist has captured men, women and children dancing.

"These paintings must be really old," Matilda says, "but the colors are so bright. I've seen cave paintings in Australia similar to this, but they're always much fainter."

Then, past the picture of the people dancing, towards the far end of the wall, you see a picture of the apprentice. He is with two other people. Your mouth drops open and your hand slowly rises to point at the image. "Matilda, look! It's—it's us! The clothes are the same and the hair color, and the…"

You can see a full circle of white around Matilda's pupils when she sees the part of the painting you're indicating.

"Bleedin' heck! How is that possible?"

"I thought I'd arrive a little earlier and record our visit," a voice from the darkness says. The apprentice steps into the light. "I see you got the fire going."

"You painted that?" you ask. "But when?"

The apprentice laughs. "You don't understand space-time very well do you? I just set the sorcerer's time machine to drop me off an hour earlier so I could paint in peace before you two arrived."

"Well it's a good likeness, I'll give you that," Matilda says. "But I bet you confuse the anthropologists if they ever find this place."

"Oh well, nothing like a few mysteries to keep people guessing. I drew a spaceman in the last cave I visited, that'll really get them going."

"So where are we?" you ask.

"And what year is it?" Matilda asks.

"This is a cave in France. It will be found in about 17,000 years."

"17,000 years!" Matilda cries. "How are we going to get home from here?"

"Don't worry. Answer this next question right, and you'll be nearly home."

You shoot the apprentice a suspicious look. "You said that last time."

"It's true," the apprentice says. "You just have to get the answer right, that's all."

You kick the ground. "Okay, but how about something easy for a change?"

"I'll see what I can do. If I give you an easy question, and you get it wrong, I'll have to send you all the way back to the beginning of the maze. You sure you want that?"

"All the way back?" you ask.

"That's not a fair suck of the sav," Matilda says.

The apprentice looks confused and turns toward you. "Translation?" he says.

"It's unfair. She doesn't like it," you say.

"Sorry, Matilda. I don't make the rules," the apprentice says.

You turn and face Matilda. "What do you think? Should we go for an easy one?"

"Give it a go, mate. We're 17,000 years from home. How much worse could it get?"

You glance at the apprentice. "You did say easy didn't you?"

"Yes but 'easy' is a relative term. For a monkey, climbing a tree is easy, but for an elephant ... not so much." The apprentice gives you a smile. "So, are you a monkey or an elephant?"

You're not really sure what monkeys and elephants have to do with this decision, but you do like climbing trees. Maybe that's a clue. You scratch your head and think a moment.

"Come on ya galah. Go for it." Matilda urges.

"Okay," you say to the apprentice. "We'll go for it."

"Right … here we go. This cave painting is in France. But where is France?"

Is France in South America? **P88**

Or

Is France in Europe? **P83**

Nearly home

"Well done," the apprentice says once the mist has cleared. "You've only got one more question to answer correctly and you get to go home."

"It's about time," Matilda says. "I'm so peckish I could eat the foot off a low flying duck."

The apprentice looks at you with a confused expression on his face. "Translation?"

"She's very, very hungry," you say, shaking your head. "Don't worry, you get used to it after a while."

Ignoring Matilda, you scan the countryside. Gently rolling hills covered with green grass and sheep rise off into the distance. A few craggy old trees dot the ridgeline.

You glance over at the apprentice. "Where are we? And where did all these sheep come from?"

"Ah ha," the apprentice says. "That is a very good question."

"If I figure it out, will we get to go home?" you ask

"At least there's lots to eat if we get stuck," Matilda says eying up the nearest sheep. "Baaaaa!" she bleats. "Baaaaaaa!"

The sheep glances up from its grassy meal, takes one look at Matilda, and races off to join the rest of the flock.

"Go on, run!" Matilda yells after the startled beast. "But remember, I know where you live!"

"Do you always have that effect on sheep, Matilda?" you ask, trying not to laugh.

"Sheep and young children," Matilda answers with a

straight face.

The apprentice covers his mouth to stifle a laugh. "Ahem… So, are you ready for your last question?"

You nod. "Ready as I'll ever be I guess."

The apprentice reaches into his pocket and pulls out a piece of paper. "Right here are a few hints. All you've got to do it tell me which country we're in. But be careful. Get it wrong and I'll have to spin the dial and send you off to who knows where."

He hands you the paper.

Hint one: This country has the southernmost capital city in the world. Hint two: This country is home to the giant weta, the world's largest insect. Hint three: bungee jumping began here.

So where are you?"

Chile **P26**

New Zealand **P98**

South Africa **P62**

Argentina **P78**

You have chosen glacial meringue

"Oops," the apprentice says. "That's not right. A meringue is a sweet dessert made by whipping egg whites and sugar together. While a moraine is the pile of rocks pushed along by a glacier and then left behind when it retreats. Because you got that wrong, I've got to spin the dial and see where we end up."

"Great," Matilda says, scratching under her robe. "Then maybe we can lose these manky furs. I think you missed a flea or two."

The mention of fleas has you scratching. "Yeah let's get the next question over with before a dinosaur comes along and eats us."

The apprentice shakes his head. "Don't be silly. The dinosaurs died out around 65 million years ago. You might get trampled by a wooly mammoth or get eaten by a saber-toothed tiger, but you won't find any dinosaurs except as fossils."

"Saber-toothed tiger? You mean like Diego in that movie *Ice Age*?" Matilda asks.

"Yep. Did you know they had teeth almost 12 inches long?" the apprentice asks.

"Crikey!" Matilda says. "That's not a tooth, that's a foot! Spin that dial and let's get the heck out of here. I'm too young to be cat food."

"Okay, hold tight." He turns the dial.

BANG—FLASH!

The shock nearly knocks you off your feet. "Whoa that was a big one!" you say, regaining your balance and looking around. "Where are we? I smell fart."

"It's not fart," the apprentice says holding his nose and speaking like he's got a cold, "it's sulphur."

"Sulphur?" you repeat.

The apprentice nods. "We're in New Zealand. You know, where they filmed *Lord of the Rings*. We're just outside a town called Rotorua."

"Jeez… You mean people have to smell fart all the time?" Matilda says. "And I though using the bathroom after my dad was bad."

"You don't notice it after a while," the apprentice says. "Or so they say."

"Yuck," you say. "I can taste it in the air. Can you please give us another question before I choke?"

"Don't you want to know about New Zealand? It has

geysers and volcanoes. You can ski on them you know."

"Ski on a geyser?" Matilda says.

"No, the volcanoes," the apprentice says. "Stop being a drongo."

"I'm not a bird," Matilda says. "We have spangled drongos back home in Australia." She tucks her hands under her armpits and starts flapping her elbows like a demented chicken. "Nope, I can't fly either. Definitely not a drongo."

The apprentice rolls his eyes then reaches for his pocket. "Okay here's an easy one. If you get this wrong you've got to go back to the very beginning of the maze. But, if you get it right, you'll be nearly home. How does that sound?"

You nod. The smell in the air is getting to you. Despite having your hand over your mouth and nose, your eyes are beginning to water. "Go for it," you say quickly, before replacing your hand.

"Okay. Here we go," the apprentice says. "What are New Zealanders known as? Are they called:"

Kiwis after a flightless bird? **P83**

Or

Wallabies after the marsupial? **P78**

Back in time

"It's dark," Matilda says. "Where are we?"

"I think we're in a cave," you reply.

Standing quietly as your eyes adjust, you listen to the sounds around you. Somewhere further into the cave you hear the steady *plonk, plonk, plonk* of water dripping.

After a minute or so, you start to see shadows. A small amount of light is seeping into the cave through a crack high in the rock above you. Wisps of smoke drift up from the remnants of a fire inside a semicircle of rocks built up against one wall.

"Someone's been down here," you say. "And they haven't been gone very long by the looks of those ashes."

"Where's the apprentice?" Matilda asks, looking around nervously. "I hope he's not too far, it's chilly down here and

I'm a bit claustrophobic."

Next to the makeshift fireplace is a pile of branches. You kneel down on the ground and blow on the embers. A couple pieces glow red.

"I'll see if I can get this fire going," you say. "It'll warm us up and give us some light while we figure out what to do."

You grab one of the smaller branches and break it into pieces. These you lay gently over the embers.

"Don't smother it, mate," Matilda says. "It needs air to burn."

You purse you lips and blow. The extra oxygen makes the embers glow red-hot and before you know it, the small pile of kindling bursts into flames. Slowly, you add more twigs and branches to the growing fire.

It isn't until you look up from your task that you spot the paintings on the wall behind you.

"Whoa!" you say taking in the scene. "Matilda, look behind you!"

Matilda turns. Her eyes widen. "That's amazing!"

Matilda isn't exaggerating. The back wall of the cave, opposite the fire, is covered in simple, yet beautiful paintings. Images of deer, horses and other grazing animals stretch from one side of the cave to the other. One animal looks a bit like a giraffe. In the centre of the wall is a painting of a fire, not unlike your own. Around it, the artist has captured men, women and children dancing.

"These paintings must be really old," Matilda says, "but the colors are so bright. I've seen cave paintings in Australia similar to this, but they're always much fainter."

Then, past the picture of the people dancing, towards the far end of the wall, you see a picture of the apprentice. He is with two other people. Your mouth drops open and your hand slowly rises to point at the image. "Matilda, look! It's—it's us! The clothes are the same and the hair color, and the…"

You can see a full circle of white around Matilda's pupils when she sees the part of the painting you're indicating.

"Bleedin' heck! How is that possible?"

"I thought I'd arrive a little earlier and record our visit," a voice from the darkness says. The apprentice steps into the light. "I see you got the fire going."

"You painted that?" you ask. "But when?"

The apprentice laughs. "You don't understand space-time very well do you? I just set the sorcerer's time machine to drop me off an hour earlier so I could paint in peace before you two arrived."

"Well it's a good likeness, I'll give you that," Matilda says. "But I bet you confuse the anthropologists if they ever find this place."

"Oh well, nothing like a few mysteries to keep people guessing. I drew a spaceman in the last cave I visited, that'll really get them going."

"So where are we?" you ask.

"And what year is it?" Matilda asks.

"This is a cave in France. It will be found in about 17,000 years."

"17,000 years!" Matilda cries. "How are we going to get home from here?"

"Don't worry. Answer this next question right, and you'll be nearly home."

You shoot the apprentice a suspicious look. "You said that last time."

"It's true," the apprentice says. "You just have to get the answer right, that's all."

You kick the ground. "Okay, but how about something easy for a change?"

"I'll see what I can do. If I give you an easy question, and you get it wrong, I'll have to send you all the way back to the beginning of the maze. You sure you want that?"

"All the way back?" you ask.

"That's not a fair suck of the sav," Matilda says.

The apprentice looks confused and turns toward you. "Translation?" he says.

"It's unfair. She doesn't like it," you say.

"Sorry, Matilda. I don't make the rules," the apprentice says.

You turn and face Matilda. "What do you think? Should we go for an easy one?"

"Give it a go, mate. We're 17,000 years from home. How much worse could it get?"

You glance at the apprentice. "You did say easy didn't you?"

"Yes but 'easy' is a relative term. For a monkey, climbing a tree is easy, but for an elephant ... not so much." The apprentice gives you a smile. "So, are you a monkey or an elephant?"

You're not really sure what monkeys and elephants have to do with this decision, but you do like climbing trees. Maybe that's a clue. You scratch your head and think a moment.

"Come on ya galah. Go for it." Matilda urges.

"Okay," you say to the apprentice. "We'll go for it."

"Right … here we go. This cave painting is in France. But where is France?"

Is France in South America? **P88**

Or

Is France in Europe? **P83**

Back at the laboratory

Oops!! How did that happen?

It's as if time has reversed and you're back in the lab.

"Hey, Matilda," you say over your shoulder, "looks like I got that last question wrong. We're back at the beginning of the maze."

"Oh well," she says with a shrug. "At least it will give us a chance to look at all this equipment a bit more."

Matilda scurries down between two rows of benches. "Now where was that time machine?" She mumbles. "Ah there it is."

"Matilda! Not again. You'll get us in trouble."

Matilda ignores you and starts fiddling with the dial.

"That's a bad idea," you say. "You know what happened last—"

FLASH—BANG!

"Crikey!" Matilda says with a shake of her head. "I'll never get used to that noise."

Once again the air is full of mist and Matilda looms ghostlike through the haze.

"Welcome back to 2560 B.C," the apprentice says. "Miss me?" He reaches out his hand. "You'd better give me that box, Matilda, before you do something silly."

You glare at your Australian friend. "You mean like sending us back to Egypt…AGAIN!"

"Sorry," Matilda says, blushing slightly. "I just thought—"

"Just stop!" you say, cutting her off. "Is there anything you can do?" you ask the apprentice. "My friend here isn't the brightest bulb in the box."

"Sorry, I don't make up the rules. You'll have to go thought the maze again."

Matilda smiles. "Hey lighten up. This is fun. Any chance of getting something to eat while we're here?"

"Are you *always* hungry?" the apprentice asks.

She shakes her head. "Not always, mate. Just most of the time. In fact I was once so hungry I barbequed a goanna."

"You mean those big lizards?" you ask.

"Yup," Matilda says, giving you a cheeky grin. "Tasted a bit like chicken."

The apprentice tucks the black box under his arm and reaches into his pocket for a question. "I don't think there are goannas around here. Let's try a question, maybe we'll get lucky."

"Sounds good to me," you say. "Time travel makes me hungry too. But I'm not eating goanna."

"I'm not a fan of barbequed reptile either," the apprentice says, holding up a small scrap of paper. "Okay. Here is an easy one. What is the only country that is an island AND a continent? Is it:"

Australia? **P26**

Or

China? **P40**

There are 1400 seconds in one hour

"Oh dear," the apprentice says. "Now you're in for it."

"Why?" you ask, "Just because my math isn't so good?"

"No, because you didn't think to use a calculator, or a computer or something to help you out. You just guessed didn't you?"

"Yeah well—"

"Does that mean we miss out on ice cream?" Matilda asks, giving you a nasty look. "Mate! What were you thinking?"

"Sorry, Matilda. I just—"

"—hey it's all right," the apprentice says. "You'll get another chance."

Matilda smiles. "Will we?"

The apprentice nods. "I'll just ask you another question

about time. If you get it right, you can have ice cream. How does that sound?"

You wipe the sweat off your forehead. Matilda can be such a pain at times. The last thing you need is her on your back. "And if I get it wrong?" you ask.

"Well, let's just say, ice cream won't be on the menu."

"Now think hard!" Matilda says. "I'll die if I don't get some ice cream soon."

"Stop it!" you say. "How am I supposed to think with you pressuring me?"

Matilda kicks the ground. "Sorry, mate. As you were."

"Okay," the apprentice says. "Now that you two have got that out of the way. Which of the following statements is correct?"

Watches were invented in Germany. **P83**

Or

Watches were invented in Australia. **P78**

Welcome to the sorcerer's office

You find yourself in a room filled with books. It's a room unlike any you've ever seen. Your eyes are drawn upward, higher and higher.

"These shelves must be a hundred feet high," you say, craning your neck to see the top.

There is no ceiling. The room is open to the sky. You can see birds circling in the sunshine and white fluffy clouds drifting by.

"Holy moly!" Matilda says tilting her head back. "Is this place awesome, or what?"

"Ahem," a voice says, bringing your view back to floor level. "So you like my office?"

Through its last few wisps of mist, you see the sorcerer's apprentice sitting behind a large wooden desk. He is wearing brightly colored robes and a pointy hat with stars and planets on it.

"Your office?" you say. "Pretty awesome office for an apprentice!"

Matilda reaches over and pulls a book from the shelf. *"The Sorcerer's Maze Jungle Trek,"* she reads. "Is this one of yours?"

The apprentice nods. "They're all mine. Your adventure will be written up some day too. But before we get sidetracked, I'd better get you home."

"You're sending us home?" Matilda asks, putting the book back. "But don't we get to meet the sorcerer?"

The apprentice snaps his fingers and two big armchairs appear. "Please have a seat. I've got something I need to tell you."

Once you and Matilda are comfortable, the apprentice snaps his fingers again and a tray of snacks appear on a small table in front of you.

"Chocolate?" the apprentice says. "Pretzels? You must be hungry after your journey."

Matilda doesn't need to be asked twice. She grabs a big handful of pretzels. "Mmmmm, thanks," she mumbles after stuffing a couple in her mouth.

The chocolate looks good, but at this point in time, you're more interested in what happens next. "So you'll send us home?" you say, repeating Matilda's question. "Where's the sorcerer? You said we'd get to meet him once we got through the maze."

"I am the sorcerer."

"Puwah!" Matilda spits pretzel crumbs everywhere.

"You?" you say. "But I thought—"

"—I was just an apprentice?"

"Yeah, well…"

The sorcerer smiles. "Sorry for the confusion. Normally I *would* send an apprentice out with my guests to accompany them through the maze, but I'm so short staffed at the moment I had to come out on this trip myself. I don't suppose you'd be interested in a job?"

You study the boy's expression and try to figure out if he's joking. "Me? A sorcerer's apprentice?"

He nods. "Yes, you. Your job will be to help me make up questions for my mazes.

By now Matilda has recovered. "So you've been lying to us? That's not very nice."

"Well technically I wasn't actually lying. You see, I cast a spell on myself so I'd act just like an apprentice while we were in the maze. I didn't want to spoil your experience you see. It wasn't until I got back to my office here, that I turned back into my real self."

Matilda's face scrunches up in confusion. She looks unconvinced. "Hang on, mate! If you—"

The sorcerer leans towards Matilda, peers deeply into her eyes. "Okay, I'm sorry. I shouldn't have lied."

Matilda thinks a moment, and then smiles. "Apology accepted." She picks up another pretzel. "Great nibbles by the way."

The sorcerer turns and gives you a grin. "Chocolate?"

"Did you just put a spell on Matilda?"

"No. What makes you think that?"

You study the sorcerer's face. His gaze is steady and looks directly at you. You've heard people who are lying often can't look you in the eye.

"Okay if you're sure…"

The sorcerer smiles.

Feeling better, you reach out and take some chocolate. But as the rich creamy lump melts in your mouth, you feel your eyelids drooping. It's been a long day and you're sure it's well past your normal bedtime.

*****

The next morning, when you wake up, a faint pink mist fills your bedroom and the book you were reading rests on the bed beside you. Was it all just a dream? Or did you really work your way through the sorcerer's maze?

As you ponder this question, your phone rings. You pick it up from your bedside table and swipe the screen. "Hello?"

"Is that you?" Matilda says, on the other end of the line.

"Yeah it's me. What's up?"

"Mate! You're not going to believe the dream I had last night!"

"Oh I think I might," you say.

"Ya reckon? Okay smarty-pants, have a guess then. What was it about?"

You hesitate a moment pretending to think. "Did you visit ancient Egypt by any chance, or meet a sorcerer? Did you have to answer questions to get home again?"

"Crikey!" Matilda says. "Now how the heck did you know that?"

THE END

Do you want to read some free previews? **P108**

Or

Would you like to check out the List of Choices to check and see if you've missed parts of the story? **P104**

Please remember to review this book on Amazon.com

This helps the authors and lets other readers know if the book is right for them. It only takes a minute and reviews don't have to be long.

Thanks,

The Sorcerer

LIST OF CHOICES

Bonus Preview: The Sorcerer's Maze Adventure Quiz

Enter the Maze

Your feet are sinking into a marshmallow floor.

You take a few quick steps and find you can stay on top if you keep moving. How did you get here? One moment you were reading and now you're in a long hallway. The place smells of candy and the pink walls are soft when you poke them.

There is a sign hanging from the ceiling that says:

THE BEGINNING OF THE SORCERER'S MAZE.

But how do you get through to the end of the maze?

Down at the end of the hallway is an old red door. Maybe you should start there?

You take a few bouncy steps, your arms held out to help keep your balance. Getting up would be hard. You don't want to fall.

At last, you make it to the red door and try the doorknob. It's locked. You pace in a circle to stop from sinking. When you turn back to the door, you find another sign. On this sign is a question. Below the question are two possible answers. Maybe answering the question correctly will let you open the door.

The questions reads: What is the largest planet in our solar system?

It's time to make your first decision.

You may pick right, you may pick wrong, but still the story will go on.

What shall it be? Is it:

Jupiter?

Or

Saturn?

Bonus Preview: The Sorcerer's Maze Jungle Trek

Enter the Jungle Maze

One moment you were at home reading a book and now you're standing in the jungle, deep in the Amazon rainforest.

Beside you flows a slow-moving river, murky brown from all the silt it carries downstream. Monkeys screech in the tall trees across the water. The air is hot and buzzing with insects. As you watch, the tiny flying creatures gather together in an unnatural cloud formation and then separate to form words:

WELCOME, they spell in giant letters.

You blink once, then again. This is crazy.

NOPE, IT'S NOT CRAZY, spell the insects. THIS IS THE START OF THE SORCERER'S MAZE.

The insect cloud bursts apart and the tiny creatures buzz off. What's next?

Twenty yards away, two kids, about your age, stand beside a small boat with a little outboard motor attached to its stern, and a blue roof to protect its occupants from the hot tropical sun.

They both smile and wave.

The girl walks towards you. "Do you want a ride upriver?" she asks. "My brother and I know the Amazon well."

"Do you work for the sorcerer?" you ask. "He designed the maze, didn't he?"

The girl nods. "Yes. My brother and I are his apprentices. The sorcerer wants you to have company while you're here."

As the two of you move down the bank to the river's edge, the girl points to the boy. "This is Rodrigo. I'm Maria."

You drop your daypack into the boat and hold out your hand. "Hi Rodrigo, interesting looking boat."

Rodrigo shakes your hand. "It does the job. But before we can go upriver," he says, pulling a piece of paper out of his pocket. "The sorcerer wants me to ask you a question. If you get it right, we can leave."

"And if not?" you ask.

"I've got more questions," the boy says, patting his pocket. "I'm sure you'll get one right eventually." Rodrigo unfolds the paper. "Okay, here's your first question. Which of the following statements is true?"

It is time to make a choice. Which do you choose?

The Amazon River has over 3000 species of fish.

Or

The Amazon River has less than 1000 species of fish.

More 'You Say Which Way' Adventures

Danger on Dolphin Island
Pirate Island
In the Magician's House
Creepy House
Dragons Realm
Stranded Starship
Dungeon of Doom
Volcano of Fire
Secrets of Glass Mountain
Mystic Portal
Dinosaur Canyon
Deadline Delivery
Between The Stars
Lost in Lion Country
Once Upon an Island
Danger on Dolphin Island
Island of Giants
The Sorcerer's Maze Jungle Trek
The Sorcerer's Maze Adventure Quiz

Printed in Great Britain
by Amazon

78333090R00072